W9-AJL-179
JEFFERSONVILLE TOWNSHIP PUBLIC LIBRARY
JEFFERSONVILLE, INDIANA
OCT -- 1999

To Brenda and Stephen — M. W.

To my sister, Anne — S. M.

First U.S. edition 1999

Library of Congress Cataloging-in-Publication Data

Waddell, Martin.
The hollyhock wall / written by Martin Waddell ; illustrated by Salley Mavor.—1st U.S. ed.
p. cm.
Summary: After Mary makes a garden in an old cooking pot and includes in it a
boy fashioned out of clay, she finds herself with him in the garden.
ISBN 1-56402-902-6
[1. Gardens—Fiction. 2. Dreams—Fiction. 3. Imagination—Fiction.] I. Mavor, Salley, ill. II. Title.
PZ7.W1137Ho 1999 [E]—dc21 97-31631

2 4 6 8 10 9 7 5 3 1

Printed in Hong Kong

Illustrator's note: "I like to make pictures out of things I can touch. Scraps of cloth, wood, and wire are hand sewn with thread to make parts of the picture. Then the trees, houses, and stuffed people are stitched to a cloth background. Sometimes I use objects that I've found, such as an old watch, a broken belt buckle, or real growing plants."

The pictures were photographed for color transparencies by Doug Mindell.
This book was typeset in Gararond Bold.

Candlewick Press
2067 Massachusetts Avenue
Cambridge, Massachusetts 02140

The Hollyhock Wall

Martin Waddell
illustrated by Salley Mavor

CANDLEWICK PRESS
CAMBRIDGE, MASSACHUSETTS

THERE ONCE WAS A GIRL who lived with her mother at the top of a very tall house.

"I wish I had a garden to play in," she told her mother.

"Why not make one, Mary?" said her mother, and she brought the girl an old cooking pot from the kitchen.

Together they filled it with earth, and the girl planted seeds in the garden and waited.

TIMEX

The seeds grew, some into grass, some into flowers, and some into trees that stood at one end of the garden. I don't know what sort of trees they were, but they *looked* like trees in the woods.

The girl made a path of small stones, and a pool fed by a stream of bright blue ribbon. Over the stream was a bridge made from matches.

She painted a hollyhock wall around the rim of the pot, a wall that ran right around her garden. But no one lived there, and the garden seemed lonely and sad.

"I'll make a boy and put him in my garden," the girl said. She made him of clay and gave him a clay wheelbarrow with a brown button wheel.

"I think his name's Tom," said the girl. "But he's bored. He's got nothing to do."

"Perhaps he could fish in the stream," said her mother.

So the little girl made a rod from a match. She fitted fine thread for a line and made a hook from part of a pin. It looked *almost* real to the girl, and Tom didn't know any better, for he'd never been fishing before.

"Tom's caught no fish," said the girl.

"There are no fish to catch," said her mother. "Better not tell him."

"I'll make Tom some fish," said the girl.

She cut silver paper into fish shapes, and she put the fish in the stream.

"That's done and Tom's pleased," said the girl. "But he needs someone to play with."

"Not tonight," said her mother.

"Why not?" said the girl.

"Because he's going to bed, just like you," said her mother.

But her mother was wrong.

The girl went to bed, but Tom didn't.

Tom stood on the bridge and he fished in the dark, though I don't think he caught much, for the fish didn't rise. They weren't *real* fish, so they couldn't.

The girl climbed out of bed and went back to play with her garden. She knelt beside the garden and looked over the hollyhock wall to see how the garden would look if it were a real garden, and big.

But somehow,
some strange how,
something strange
happened . . .

Somehow the girl was there in her garden, over the hollyhock wall, among the tall trees in the woods.

She met Tom, pushing his wheelbarrow.

"Hello, Tom," said the girl.

"I'm glad you are here," said the boy. "I've been waiting for you; I've no one to play with. Will you play with me?"

"Yes, please," said the girl.

They played in the woods. They splashed in the pool. They fished for bright fish from the bridge. Then they cooked the fish on a fire made from sticks, and they drank the clear water that flowed in the stream.

"Let's play tag," said the girl.
They chased around the garden, one after the other, and Tom ran down the path by the hollyhock wall.

"Don't climb over the hollyhock wall!" cried the girl. "You'll fall out of the pot."

"What pot?" asked Tom.

"This one," said the girl. "The one that we're in. The pot on the table that sits in my room."

Tom didn't believe her. He jumped right over the hollyhock wall.

And somehow,
some strange how,
something strange
happened again,
but it happened the
other way around. . .

The girl was back in her room, looking over the hollyhock wall.

Small Tom lay on the table, just by the pot.

"Tom," said the girl, but Tom didn't speak. She'd made him out of clay, and clay doesn't talk.

The girl put Tom back on the bridge, and she fetched his wheelbarrow from the woods and put it beside him.

I must have dreamed it, she thought;
and maybe she had,
or maybe not.

But that's not the end of the story.

The next day her mother looked at the garden.

"You made a girl just like you," said her mother.

"Well, maybe I did," said the girl, feeling confused, for maybe she had, but she didn't know when she had done it.

"What will you call her?" her mother asked.

"I think she is Mary, like me," said the girl. She knew that she was the girl in the garden, though she didn't know how she could be.

"Now Tom has someone to play with," her mother said.

Mary knelt on the floor, looking into the garden at the two people made of clay. They did nothing at all. How could they?

The strange thing never happened again, but somehow,

some strange how,

something else happened . . .

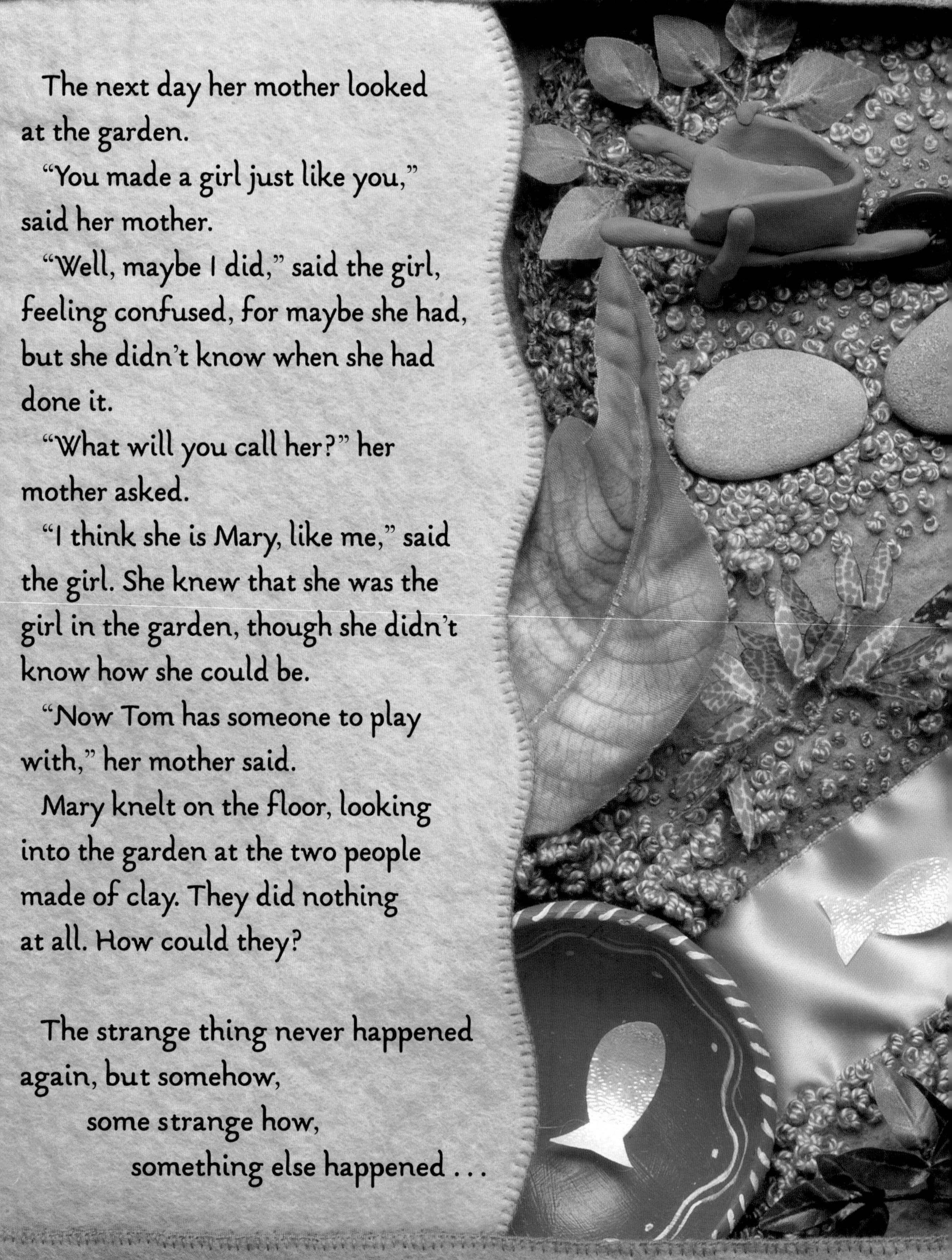

The girl went to stay at her granny's new house, and the house had a garden. She ran down the garden and came to a hollyhock wall.

She looked over the wall at the garden next door.

Somehow she knew what she'd see.

There were tall trees and a stream and a pond and a boy who was pushing a wheelbarrow.

"Tom," the girl called. "Do you know who I am?"

The boy smiled and held out his hand. "Yes, I do," said Tom. "You're Mary."

And they played all day in the garden.